DUCK, in the TRUCK

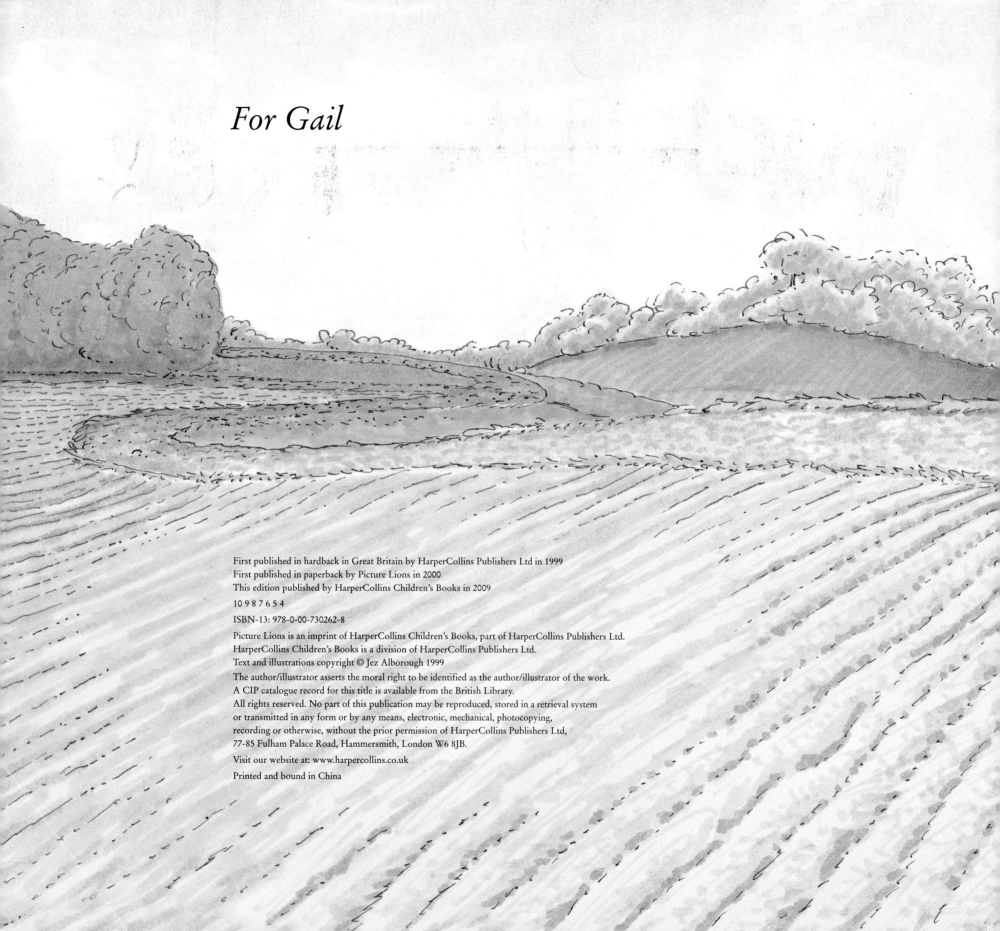

For Gail

First published in hardback in Great Britain by HarperCollins Publishers Ltd in 1999
First published in paperback by Picture Lions in 2000
This edition published by HarperCollins Children's Books in 2009
10 9 8 7 6 5 4
ISBN-13: 978-0-00-730262-8
Picture Lions is an imprint of HarperCollins Children's Books, part of HarperCollins Publishers Ltd.
HarperCollins Children's Books is a division of HarperCollins Publishers Ltd.
Text and illustrations copyright © Jez Alborough 1999
The author/illustrator asserts the moral right to be identified as the author/illustrator of the work.
A CIP catalogue record for this title is available from the British Library.
Visit our website at: www.harpercollins.co.uk
Printed and bound in China

DUCK in the TRUCK

Jez Alborough

HarperCollins Children's Books

This is the Duck driving home in a truck.

This is the track which is taking him back.

This is the rock struck by the truck   and this is

the muck   where the truck becomes stuck.

These are the feet which
jump the Duck down

into the muck
all yucky and brown.

This is the frog who
spies from the bush

and croaks, "I'll help you
give it a push!"

This is the push of a Frog   and a Duck…

And this is the truck still stuck.

This is a sheep
driving home in a jeep.

"Get out of the way,"
he yells with a beep.

This is the quack of an angry Duck.
"I can't," he snaps, "my truck is stuck."

This is the
quiet…

...as they think
what to do.

"Got it!" croaks Frog,
Sheep can push too."

This is the slurp　　　and squelch　　　and suck

as the Sheep steps slowly through the muck.

This is the push of a Sheep, a Frog   and a Duck

and this is the truck... still stuck.

This is the happy sleepy Goat
relaxing on his motorboat.

This is the ear that
hears the shout,

"My truck's in the muck
and it won't come out!"

This is the rope
and here's the Goat's plan,

to tie a knot
as tight as they can.

This is the push at the rear once again.

This is the pull as the boat takes the strain.

These are
the wheels

finally
gripping.

TWANG

This is
the knot

suddenly
slipping.

This is the truck with the engine on fast

back on the truck…   UNSTUCK AT LAST!

This is the Duck driving home in the truck

leaving the Frog, the Sheep and the Goat…

STUCK IN THE MUCK!